Turkey Tumble

by Jonah Newman

Illustrated by Paul Nicholls

Scholastic Inc.

ISBN 978-1-338-59207-8

10 9 8 7   20 21 22 23

Printed in the U.S.A.   40
First printing 2019

Illustrated by Paul Nicholls
Book design by Lizzy Yoder

It was the day of the harvest,
and all through the wood,
the animals were working
to make the feast good.
But two of the creatures
weren't helping at all.
Instead they were talking
about topics quite small.

There were three busy bunnies,
arranging things with glee . . .

Below two chatty turkeys,
talking in a tree.

There were four helpful hedgehogs,
pouring mugs of tea . . .
Next to three busy bunnies,

below two chatty turkeys,
talking in a tree.

There were five furry foxes, baking bread with ease . . .

Near four helpful hedgehogs, three busy bunnies, below two chatty turkeys, talking in a tree.

There were six speedy squirrels,
on a spending spree . . .

There were seven merry mice,
bringing plates of cheese . . .

To six speedy squirrels,
five furry foxes,
four helpful hedgehogs,
three busy bunnies,

below two chatty turkeys, talking in a tree.

There were eight cheerful
chipmunks, kindly asking please . . .
To seven merry mice,
Six speedy squirrels,

Five furry foxes,
Four helpful hedgehogs,
Three busy bunnies,

Below two chatty turkeys,
talking in a tree.

There were nine baby bears,
serving food for free . . .
To eight cheerful chipmunks,
Seven merry mice,

Six speedy squirrels,
Five furry foxes,
Four helpful hedgehogs,
Three busy bunnies,

There were ten big-toothed beavers,
gnawing through the tree . . .

With nine baby bears, serving food for free,

Eight cheerful chipmunks, kindly asking please,

Seven merry mice, bringing plates of cheese,

Six speedy squirrels, on a spending spree,

Five furry foxes, baking bread with ease,

Four helpful hedgehogs, pouring mugs of tea,

Three busy bunnies, arranging things with glee . . .

Below two chatty turkeys,

WOBBLE!

WOBBLE!

The two chatty turkeys
Fell hard and fell fast.

They landed right on the table
With an almighty
CRASH!

The friends looked around
At the mess from the birds.
The table was broken.
Their meal looked absurd!

They greeted their guests,
Despite their surprise.
A brave bear spoke up . . .